Our Story Retold

The Black Experience Unveiled Through Poetry

CLAION B. GRANDISON

First published in Great Britain in 2024 by Made For Ministry Ltd

Publisher:
Made For Ministry Ltd
6-9 Union St
Luton
LU1 3AN
United Kingdom
Web: www.madeforministry.com
Email: hello@madeforministry.com

Hardback ISBN: 978-1-0687652-1-6
Paperback ISBN: 978-1-0687652-0-9

Contents Page

Dedication

This book is lovingly dedicated to my amazing parents; Phillip Benjamin who passed away 1st April 2019 age 96 and Adassa Grandison 93.

To my wonderful children Samara and Zephan the greatest gifts a father could be given.

To Sonia my wife and best friend, the strongest and funniest woman I know, "I adore you".

To all my fellow poets, critics and encouragers who affirmed my early attempts at writing in rhythmic rhyme, you are priceless.

Finally I give God thanks for His gift that came quite unexpectedly, and subsequently became a blessing to so many around the world.

Claion

Foreword

To be a pastor and a poet is a rare thing. But I will admit I was not at all surprised when Bishop Claion first told me about his upcoming poetry book. Unsurprised because the deep love that Bishop Claion has for God and for people cannot be contained, I think only in sermons. Unsurprised because Bishop Claion is unafraid of emotion and tears – I am yet to have a conversation that does not at some point, lead him to remove his glasses and reach for a tissue. As you will find in this collection, he is brave and strong enough to tell the truth about the beauty and the difficulty of our human experience and our lives of faith.

This collection of poems from a spiritual father (again these are rare) is born out of love, particularly for black people, and especially the stories not often told among our communities. There are healing words for those of us who have never heard 'thank you' or 'I am sorry' when we should have, those whose beauty is overlooked and whose gifts are unrecognised and stifled. There is encouragement, for those of us who wonder if we are loveable, those who have felt or feel abandoned, and those who wonder what to do with their regrets and disappointments.

This spiritual and creative book honours so many of the joys and struggles we experience as Black Caribbeans in Britain. Poems are dedicated to children who came to join their families in the UK from the Caribbean, to survivors of domestic abuse, and to the pastors whose integrity and labours go unnoticed and underappreciated. There are poems inspired by important figures in Bishop Claion's own life including his wife Sonia, his parents and community leaders he has encountered. A love poem to NTCG is a beautiful addition.

But the poems also reflect the social issues of our day including violence on UK streets and incidents of racist violence in the US. Black lives matter and famous black figures such as Meghan Markle and Michelle Obama feature. Windrush history and colonialism are not forgotten, nor the treatment of Black British footballers. The poems in this collection recognise the challenges many of us face. Black people are seen, and considered deeply throughout these poems.

This book is important for all those who understand the spiritual importance of poetry and the arts in general. Poetry is found throughout the bible, and this anthology is a reminder that God can speak to us through many more forms than we sometimes imagine. In this collection, Bishop Claion reimagines well-known biblical texts, bringing to life stories which are familiar but can still yield wisdom and hope through this particularly creative expression. Through these poems, we might be built up, inspired, encouraged and grow in love as we seek to better understand and care for the Black women who love and nurture us. Ultimately, through this, we learn more about God who gives rest to those who carry the heaviest burdens.

Selina Stone *(Birmingham, UK, July 2024)*

Endorsements

Tedroy Powell

"Through these informative, and inspirational poems Bishop Claion Grandison has creatively connected to the vena cava of black anthropology. Although we see despair through hegemonic practices, a raging epidemic and not-so-subtle racism in sport, there is a strong thread of redemptive hope on which the reader can hold in assurance."

Bishop Tedroy Powell

National Presiding Bishop, Church of God of Prophecy, U.K., Holland & Belgium

Marcia Dixon

"Claion Grandison is one of the few church leaders who write poetry and it has to be said it's very good. So…don't be surprised to find, when reading Bishop Grandison's new book of poetry that it makes you think, reflect, inspires and causes you to conclude, like me, that his poetry was not only an enjoyable uplifting read but motivating and positively impacting too."

Marcia Dixon MBE

Publisher, Keep the Faith magazine

Mike Royal

"This is the real Bishop Claion. Relevant, edgy, challenging, uncompromising. His poetry, will make you ponder, reconsider and remember. That which you buried in your subconscious, got confused in your double conscious, front of mind again this time healing, renewing, refreshing and reviving. Go with this, don't miss dis, for a balm of Gilead awaits those who care to simply tarry awhile."

Bishop Mike Royal

General Secretary, Churches Together in England

Selina Stone

"In this collection, Bishop Claion reimagines well-known biblical texts, bringing to life stories which are familiar but can still yield wisdom and hope through this particularly creative expression."

Dr Selina Stone

Author, Tarry Awhile

Ian Galloway

"Bishop Grandison writes from the deeper places. Of beauty, of suffering, of injustice and of joy. But mostly of love. Love for life, love for people, love for truth. Be ready to see. Be ready to cry. Be ready to love. "The Harvest is Ready for a preacher who Cares, Who Connects and Creates, despite all the tares." (from Hey Preacher)."

Rev Ian Galloway

Director of Free Church Formation, St John's College, Durham

First

A tribute to my daughter Samara who came into our lives
on 1st November 2000 and changed us forever.

Your Mother was the first to feel you, a gentle kick that said I'm coming and I've got plans to change you.
On the first of November I was the first to see you, your little eyes straining at the light and then we both heard you, girl did we hear you.

Mum was the first to hold you I was the first to change you right after she was first to feed you and feed you and feed you.
We were first to fall in love with you, I was probably the first to scold you mum the first to comfort you but we were both there first to protect and care for you.

You were my first love, my first try at being a father, the first good thing that came out of me my first gift to the world was you.
You were the first to call me daddy the first to make my wife a mummy, you were first.
If harm should ever come to you, I'd certainly be the first to give my life for you even though shortly after you were born mum almost lost her life for you.

Your grandad was the first to christen you I was first to baptise you and when you're 27 I might be the first to...
We were the first to love you and we'll be the last to ever stop caring for you
Long after you've left home we'll pine after you and think of you, secretly I might even cry for you.

But long before we felt you, before we 'ere' lay eyes on you
There was One who first knew you and in your mother's womb shaped you to be you
Samara Shekinah Grandison with all our hearts we love you

Mark the Perfect Woman

Dedicated to women who have been marked by circumstances, physically and emotionally and are still considered perfect by the writer.

Mark the perfect woman
She has marks all over
Stretch marks and stress marks are the marks she wears on her tanned body.
The marks beneath and to the corners of her eyes are telltale signs of a very full life

Mark the perfect woman
How many marks will you give her out of ten if she's not quite a size ten
Will you mark her down if she's a darker shade of brown, will you feature her on the cover of your monthly magazine
Marks covered by mascara or sometimes a good old church smile.
She is the original cover girl

Mark the perfect woman
But be careful not to leave another scar.
God knows she's had her share
Mark the perfect woman
Imperfectly perfect, dysfunctionally functional, as she confidently strides through life with her limp.
Her heart's in the right place as it beats within what's left of her mutilated breasts.
Marks of survival all over her chest.

Mark the perfect woman
She loves perfectly, though she is not always perfectly loved.
She has lost the ones she loves and loves the ones she's lost...perfectly.

Mark the perfect woman
Bible in one hand and grace in the other, she shows up as she gives up her time, having stayed up the night before just so she can keep up.

She's up even when she's down.
Always up to something, up for something, standing up for someone

Mark the perfect woman
Though she's still a child with a child.
She's marked for greatness despite her poor marks she will make her mark on this world.
Her mistakes in time forgotten but her perfect mark indelibly remains.

Mark the perfect woman
She's now old and grey but still perfect in every way.
Her hands shake but her soul is steady, her mind wanders but her spirit is still.
Her end is peace, she is His masterpiece marked by perfection

Windrushed Woman

A tribute to my mother born April 24, 1931, who left her island home in Jamaica in 1952.

Rushed from your village in the cockpit regions of your island home
Your delicate but sturdy frame rushes up the steps of the mother ship as friends and family wave you off to a land full of prospects, your heart filled with dreams.
"See you in a little while a year maybe two, five at the most"

As the last bastion of the Empire pulls away with its precious cargo
You stare through floods of tears as your homeland slips over the edge of the distant horizon;
And your heart sinks as you sink into the lowest dankest part of the monstrosity some dare call a cruise liner

You've been so rushed, now you're sea sick or is it homesick as you clutch firmly to the brown and white images of your three children hardly school age, standing confidently poised on chairs in lovely taffeta dresses and a smart dark suit.

It's all been such a rush one minute you were to be the first in your family to enter higher education and now you're rushing to job number two of three just to make sure your three can join you to make you all one again.

It's been such a rush as one year turns into three and three to seventeen and now seventy
So much has changed and yet so much still remains the same.
Your delicate frame now encloses a sturdy frame of mind that still manages to hold vivid memories of your island home so far away

You don't rush so much these days, time just seems to stand still as busy grand babies rush in to see you and rush out again.
Reclining in your favourite chair reminiscing and savouring your favourite tea,

you count and recount what "de good lawd above" has done.

That little brown and white image is surrounded by several other colour ones
A display of generations capped and gowned celebrating a Wind Rushed
generation that over time became the best they could be

You Are Thirty One

A Tribute to Sonia, my best friend who became my wife.

You are thirty one, my Baskin Robbins of delicious delectable desirable flavours.
The culmination of my poetic phrases
More wise than a thousand sages
Like Solomon It's taken me until now to sum up on all these pages

What virtuous really means

You are thirty one and then some
But who's counting years when each day is as precious as the next thirty one.
You with the silver hair, golden voice and bronze complexion
Price above rubies, worth above diamonds
Tell me what you're drinking as I'd sure like to try some
Forever young, you are thirty one.

Resilient and strong, beauty and braun
Is there a story behind your powerful song
Was it your brush with death not once but twice?
Is it safe to say your worship came at a price
You shout to the people "just one more praise"
One more hallelujah and we'll be done
You are thirty one.

I'm known within the gates ever since I stopped at your gate
Ever since our first date, the one where I was late.
Ever since you let me in something happened deep within
Something more than pride
Something humbling
You see me at my worst and know there's better
You see me at my best and you're really not bothered
You are Thirty One.

A woman of few words, your often excluded
But your silence golden, is never misquoted
And when you speak, those words that are few
They fill up the room, the atmosphere becomes new
Your gift makes room for you as you make room for others
Never threatened, never envious, never jealous
You are thirty one.

Ever growing always evolving you remain the same
Seasons come and go but you are unchanged, un-phased
Godliness with contentment is your greatest gain.
A life without laughter is your greatest pain.

You are indeed the stronger one
Through hardships and challenges I've watched you hold on
Holding your family while holding your own
The original queen bae, you may ascend your throne
You are thirty one

Gigi Protégée

A tribute to the late Kobe Bryan and his daughter Gigi who were tragically killed on 26th January 2020.

I wore number 2 you wore 24
I was just thirteen, you were forty one
The Gigi to your Kobe
The father who coached me.
The light to your day
Your protégée

I watched you fly when I could only crawl
You made me fly when you handed me that ball
The Gigi to your Kobe
The real shine in your trophy.
The right to your say
Your protégée

I'm on the court and now I'm unstoppable
I shoot them hoops like I'm the boss of them
The Gigi to your Kobe
A bright future before me.
The up to your lay
Your protégée

When you left the game, you left me your name
The pressure of your fame
The Gigi to your Kobe
The Legacy you gave me
The freedom to be me.
The own to your way
Your protégée

You took me to church the Sunday before

Had our last communion then He welcomed us home
The Gigi to your Kobe
An inseparable combi
The kneel to your pray
Your protégée

Today in heaven we're on a new court
Streets of gold we've learnt a new sport
The Gigi and the Kobe
Stood before the Supreme King
God is doing a new thing.
Heaven make room for more
Number 2 and 24

If I've Let You Down

An open apology to our women, for the way we've treated them and our failure to appreciate who they truly are.

If I've let you down I'm sorry
The times I caused you worry
Walked away in a hurry
Proposed to you then scurried
For all these things and much more I'm sorry

If I called your phone when you were alone
Sent you texts I don't condone
If I slid in your DM at 2 AM
Aroused your passion and never called again
Today I'm owning my sheet, my rap sheet, I've let you down and I'm sorry.

If I've lain my hands to pray
Used "spiritual" tropes to hold you prey, I'm sorry
If I've preached the word and not kept my word
Treated love as a noun and not a verb
I've let you down and I'm sorry

If I've raised my voice in anger
Raised my hand in a temper
Raised our kids in squalor
Raised our debt and then your blood pressure
It's not how I was raised, I've let you down, and I'm sorry

If I've mistaken your pain for nagging
Misunderstood your body changing
Misread you ageing as just not caring
For all the things I've missed, I'm saying
I've let you down and I'm sorry.

If I've been average when I could have been great
Held you back on account of my own shame
Talked you down from the ledge of fame
Forgive me, from today,
I'll be a better man and I'm sorry.

Instead of letting you down
I should have let down my guard
Treated you softly and not been so hard
Lifted you up and made you my world
How could I let you down when you upheld me
Talk down to you when you spoke up for me
How could I not see that by hurting you I was hurting me.
For all these broken promises, forgive me.

My Afro Is My Crown

A celebration of Black women who embrace their hair as their crown and to my wife, who temporarily lost hers to cancer, but courageously regained it.

My Afro is my crown
This dark tanned skin my gown
Fully loaded hips all round
Feet firmly on the ground
A Naturally formed Black woman

My Afro is my crown
Thick, black, gingery brown
These kinky locs have me the talk of the town
Ever since I let it down
Worked it, owned it, to the ground
Tresses intricately woven

My Afro is my crown
Watch my haters frown
Say I let myself down
When I let my hair down
But watch my lovers drown, in the sea of my enchantment
As they see my inner movement
Lit dark brown woman

My Afro is my crown
Despite the thorns on my brow
Clumps in my hand and on the ground from my fifth round of therapy
Now thinning and shorn still proudly worn, my legacy
Against the odds Black Woman

My Afro is my crown
Kings and queens are born
As I open my heart and push from my loins

As I feed from my breasts the heirs to my throne
A king beside me or on my own
Mother of creation

Your Afro is your crown
Put it up or pull it back, but never put it down
Even if they put you down
Pick yourself up, fix your crown
Make this next season your own
My melanin coated sister

Your Afro is your crown
And don't you forget it
The years our masters forbid it
Gave us a band to cover it.
Don't leave home without it
Whether you perm or straighten it, wear it.
Your symbol of defiance

Your Afro is your crown
Let me help you plait and care it
Protect from those who kill it
Who pour their poison in it
Let me show you how to grow it
Oil your roots and strengthen it
Your jewel encrusted bonnet
We crown you queen Black Woman

Good Enough?!

A tribute to FLOTUS 44, Mrs Michelle Obama, following the publication of her bestselling book, Becoming in which she asks the question of herself several times.

My hair is thick and long recoiled and strong
But am I good enough?
My lips are far from being thin, set against a backdrop of dark brown skin
But am I good enough?

I work hard, speak softly, laugh loudly, feel deeply, weep sorrowfully
But am I good enough?
Good enough for my mother
Adored by my late father
Protected by my big brother
But what about the others
Am I really good enough?

Girl from the Southside crossed over to the other side
Just a short bus ride and yet...
Because money was never enough I guess to them I wasn't good enough?
And sadly to some I wasn't hood enough.

So I did well in school, followed every rule, never suffered fools
But was I good enough?
I Climbed high, very high
Dressed well, very well
Got paid very well
So why the...
Was I not good enough?

Met the man of my dreams, confident and real, assured and at ease
but I'm still not sure if he's really good enough to make me feel, good enough.
I take a chance on love,
for once I step out of my head, into my heart and into his arms,

slowly becoming good enough.

Always pressing, no time for messing but inside I'm stressing
"Am I really good enough?"
Pressing to straighten out those kinks in my hair or is it in my head that repeat
over and over again what the press said
You'll never be good enough

I've sat with princes dined with queens
Lived in a White House while living my dreams
Today I walk into arenas and thousands scream, the hopeless believe,
the suffocated breathe
Could it be, could it really be
That I am and always have been
Good enough

Hidden Figures

A celebration of my sisters, mothers and aunties who faced with a double prejudice have continued to excel and exceed expectations.

Hidden figures
My silhouette sisters
Come take a seat with your fellow achievers
Passed over, stepped on, shunted sideways
Held back, held up and robbed of ideas
Asking patiently, when is it my time?

Hidden figures
All your curves are plain
As the arch of your spine connects nicely to your brain.
Your beautiful breasts are a treasure chest of the dreams you carry and the pride you possess.
Somehow we're running out of time.

Hidden figures
Not figure heads but heads that figure instead
Ways to get and stay ahead.
Twice denied for your melanin, feminine design
Thrice gifted from the Trinity Divine
A species ahead of her time.

Hidden figures
Yet your light shines through
The slightest of openings reveal your deep truth.
Blind men are blinded refusing to see
Deafened and muted by the sound of your speech.
We see you biding your time.

Hidden Figures
My suffragette friends you stand before horses and terrify men.

Underground railroads, Crimean war angel, Maroon rebellions
A figure of strength you liberate millions.
A force from the starting of time.

Hidden Figures
Though buried alive
Neath layers and layers you grow stronger inside.
While haters and doubters do dance on your grave
Your will to be greater is deeply engraved
With roots drawing strength from the dark under side
The day of atoning looms, blooms closer with time.

Hidden Figures
Serendipitously exposed
Doors once sealed shut, are no longer closed
Ceilings shatter as your confidence grows
Thriving in places where no one else grows.
Figures once buried now beautifully thrive
Treasures forgotten have graciously survived
The waiting is over the harvest is ripe
Figures once hidden, know now is your time.

Ugly Beauty

Dedicated to a dear friend and fellow minister grappling with the harsh realities of life, ministry and a crumbling self image.

I look in the mirror no make up on
I see my reflection, the beauty's gone
These darkened circles are not eye shadow
But vain attempts to hide my insomnia
These blood shot eyes that weep at night
Have seen too much to sleep at night
I tell myself I'm ugly

Today I'm a mess, a tangled ball of stress
Nothing matches and I could not care less
I catch you lowering your gaze from me
I guess it's just one of those days for me.
You say I've let me down
I tell myself I'm ugly

I've just got up from prayer
I haven't said a word
I know he hasn't heard
From someone who feels so ugly
I mope about all day
What's done is done I say
I keep loved ones at bay
Unless they see my ugly

Deadlines to meet not half as dead as the people I've got to meet
Spending all day on my feat
And still I'm not accomplished, not polished, and above all things not "British"
Just ugly.

They say you see me and know my name

My inner movements as plain as day
My hidden thoughts my hidden pain
My countless failures my deepest shame
Who says being flawed is not being enough
Who passed that ruling and made it law
I hear you whisper it wasn't me
And call my ugly beauty.

The Gate Crasher

A reimagining of the woman who anoints the feet of Jesus with oil from her alabaster box in the Gospel of Luke.

For years she did as her suitors said
Lay sheets of satin across her bed
They promised to be gentle but hurt her instead.
So she walked the streets not welcomed

Then one Sabbath as evening came
She encountered a man who removed her shame
Her flicker of innocence was now a flame
By a stranger who made her welcome.

She entered the home of a Pharisee
Box in hand as she knelt at his feet
Stares of contempt by the so called elite
As she broken open her gift of a fragrance sweet.
Because she was not welcome

His sweat, mixed with her tears
As she wipes away years, of pain with her hair
Kissed the feet that stood with her
And said that she was welcomed.

Days have passed since she left the room
But the smell of her worship still lingers and looms
The fragrance of honour and costly perfume
By someone who wasn't welcome.

Women of colour who are oft not welcome.
Stood in rooms with boxes unopened.
Hindered and halted by past roads taken

Break open your vials and begin your pouring
Your fragrant scent is welcome

Black Princess

Dedicated to the Duchess of Sussex.

Twinkle twinkle little sparkle
Nubian Princess Meghan Markle
Yours is the perfect end to a story,
How a mixed race girl met a prince called Harry
Fell in love and would later marry

Black princess in a white kingdom
Your heart beats loudly like Djembe drum
Calling women to rise up and become
Rightful owners to their unclaimed heirloom
Mistresses of their predestination.

Born for this role some say it "suits" you
Played with grace the way you're used to
Lived through pain as they seek to accuse you
Your freckled smile shows strength and beauty
Dripping from head to toe in melanin royalty

Those powerful shoulders they wish you'd hide
Those slender steps you take with pride
That handsome prince close to your side
That beautiful baby boy you hide.
Those palace gates better open wide
Mother Africa's coming home to reside.

Twinkle twinkle where is your sparkle
Your freckled smile our princess Markle
So many times we tried to warn you
But true love never bows to
People
Take your flight and leave this country

Make your home where you'll all be happy

Twinkle Twinkle princess Markle
You've won our hearts without a title
Long before your prince came courting
Way before that dreaded Court of public opinion
Their Royal hubris may be obscene
But in our hearts you'll still be queen

Hey Preacher

Words of encouragement to Pastors who have the responsibility of leading churches in an environment that is constantly changing and who are seeking to remain current.

Hey preacher you're more than a sermon
A thirty minute speil on a Sunday morning
More than a collar and a 3 piece suit
More than a "hamen" a holler and a hoot

Not just a title, Reverend doctor apostle
Not just a spot to park your new vehicle.
You're more than the pay that you get paid
More than the pay that you never get paid.

You ain't no part of some underground hustle.
A pimping preacher tryna prey on a sister.
Praying in pews with one eye open
Eyeing the pews as the plate be passing.

"Thus sayeth the Lord" don't make it legit.
Speaking in tongues while having a fit.
Long fancy Greek words with Hebrew thrown in
Will tickle the ears but it won't kill sin

Don't be drawn to the latest fad
Skinny tight jeans and a t-shirt to match.
Tats and drip to make you look cool
Preacher oh preacher you're nobody's fool

You're more than the spotlight that hits you on stage
The highlights and facelifts that's hiding your age
More than your channel with five thousand views.
Gucci and Vuitton and red bottom shoes

You're a voice in the wilderness with ill fitting clothes
A diet of low cost and second hand shoes
You call to repentance the ones that are lost
A seeker of sinners not a good time host.

You're filled with the Spirit from your own mother's womb.
You're the demon possessed girl that lived among tombs
You're the one who had issues that streamed down her legs
The 12 year old damsel brought back from the dead.

You're a living epistle both chapter and verse
Old and New Testament lived out in the world.
So live your best sermon and walk out the word
Declare the prophetic the world has not heard.
The Harvest is Ready for a preacher who Cares,
Who Connects and Creates, despite all the tares.

Woman at the Well

A reimagining of Jesus' encounter with a Samaritan woman in the Gospel of John.

In the noonday sun
With the others gone
I quickly run, to the well
Jaded, evaded, taunted and hated
Of a truth I know all is not well

My life's not perfect but I'm better than most
I've stolen no money and I give to the poor
But there must be more in life to unveil
The answers would all be told at the well

My stride quickly shortened as I lessened my pace
A lonesome figure had invaded my space
He was not much to look at like most other men
But he asked for a drink from our father Jacob's well

By his features I knew that he was a Jew
For they and Samaritans our dealings were few.
Our backgrounds were different I'm sure he could tell.
Then he changed the subject saying he was the well

"Well" I said thinking this man must be mad
But as he saw through me, my heart became sad
Uncovering the secrets of the husbands I had.
Things he told me I dare not tell.
What's said at the well must remain at the well.

He never once judged the colour of my skin
Thickness of my hair or my full lipped grin
His only concern was the depth of my sin

The fact that true worship was welled from within
That day with a Jew seeking water at the well

I welled up inside crying come see a man
Who looked past my culture and saw all that I am
Who spoke to my future and broke all those spells
A man I met at a Samaritan well

To my sisters whose thirst a drink cannot quench
To my mothers and daughters who've lived their own hell.
To the unfulfilled housewife to the corporate exec.
Leave your watered down existence and come drink from this well.

I Came with a Limp

Dedicated to children who eventually came from the Caribbean to join their parents with new families; the so called Barrel Children.

I was Nine years old as I limped in the cold
Having left the warm sunshine to a house filled with mould.
Wrenched from my grandma my rock and my soul
I longed for a semblance of home.

A spirited young woman quite feisty at times
The world was my oyster, just before I arrived.
You're not my mother I protested inside
As the words of another had wounded my pride.

I longed for home and my own bedroom
A cool evening breeze a bright full moon.
Friendly greetings as a neighbour walked past
Friendly greetings now a thing of the past

I grew up fast and grew up strong
Fell quickly in love and married quite young,
All along seeking to belong
Only to be told my feelings were wrong
So I sat in my silence and just carried on.

Smiling through heartache limping through pain
I longed to give life to that nine year old me.
Longing for acceptance and the right to be free
But instead you ignored and suffocated me

For years I was duped to believing your lie
This the girl who came limping is finding her stride
Silver and gold I may not have much
But the love of my girls is more than enough

For all the young girls who came with a limp
Taunted and teased for the colour of their skin.
Mocked and jeered for their thick accent
The door is wide open, for you to walk in

Run Girl Run

To a young woman, a survivor of domestic abuse, who now supports other vulnerable women and children.

Baby in one arm black bag in another she walks out into a cold November night and flees for their lives.
Run girl run or you may not survive, you might not live till your little girl's five.

Run girl run with a cheap one way ticket to anywhere for even though your feet hurt your heart's in greater pain.
Your baby's crying nappy soiled and swollen almost as large as your left eye that collided with his right fist

Run girl run and don't you dare look back with your one good eye or this time you'll be permanently blinded to the reality of your darkened past, dissuaded by some fake tears and a fake ask for your already broken hand in marriage.
Take a deep breath and run

How did you get here, when did this all begin
Was it his smile in the club, glint in his eye, that first kiss or was it way before this.
Did he say you looked all grown up in your tight school dress, only tight because money was too.
Did he think your no was a yes and did he just hear please when you said stop please?
Run girl run.

Whisper loudly, shout softly to me the things I must hear
It's hard to listen running with the wind in your ear.
Run girl run but don't run away
Run for power without having to stay
Run for office, run for cover
Run for the girl with a baby in one hand and black bag in the other.
Run to win.

The Lady Undertaker

A tribute to an amazing female funeral director who I'm yet to meet who journeyed with the bereaved during the Pandemic Covid19.

You slowly march before the remains
Top hat and tails you hold our gaze
Scores of mourners have joined the procession
Following your lead to a tranquil location
In pouring rain in icy conditions
Your poise is sure as our loved ones transition.

Today it's a mother who's burying her son
Tomorrow it's nan who'll be laid in the ground.
As grown men crumble to bury their wives
Their trembling lips and bloodshot eyes.
Your hand on our shoulder as we lower their frame
You don't make it better but you make it humane.

There aren't many like you, Black female directors
Consummate professionals our very own sisters.
While "others" will sneer as they take our money
For you it's not a job, for you it's a ministry
A labour of love as you inter the departed
You honour our dead in a way that's deserving.

I won't call your name but it means you're the greatest
So "Maximum" respect to one of our bravest
Being on the frontline while most of us shielded
You deserve an award for your "Mitchelen" standard.
Your accolades sung for your "ground breaking" service
May your days be long and your years be gracious

The Lady Undertaker

A tribute to an unsung female funeral director who [illegible] who journeyed with the bereaved during the Pandemic Covid19

You slowly march before the remains
Two hat and [illegible] you hold your gaze
[illegible]

[illegible]

[illegible]

[illegible]

Holly

Dedicated to the memory of a dear friend who passed away after a very short illness.

In you came way back in the eighties
A new recruit on management training
I asked your name you said I'm Holly
We became best friends and the rest is history

An Alpha swan and a Calabar lion
An unlikely pair an awkward union
Harbour View and Washington Gardens
A Catholic girl with this Pentecostal bredrin

We spoke for hours it cost us money
Your quest for truth this spiritual honey
Then after months of deep soul searching
You set your course on a new God journey

I watched you grow with your own anointing
You gaining friends of similar callings
Baptised afresh and filled with fire
A Holy flame encased in Holly

We grew apart but not estranged
Our love for God kept us still engaged
Serving those who came our way
Loving souls, despite their way

A mother kind and full of grace
You gave so much and still had space
And in your loss a mother gone
Though filled with grief you carried on.

Advocate for the parentless
Divine example of selflessness
Heavyweight Champion for society's reject
You contend courageously and doggedly in the ring of child neglect.

That fateful day it came too soon
A life cut short at fifty two
This graceful swan would fold her wings
Would leave this world for greater things
A faith that blossomed right to the end
Now rest in peace my forever friend

Chrisma

My farewell after 17 years to the first church I ever pastored.

No ordinary church or fly by night ministry
In 2003 begun our story
A broken church with a broken people
Broken finances and a broken building
A cold December we began our journey
And as the saying goes the rest is history

I couldn't tell you my maiden sermon
What I do recall is the place was freezing.
Some lively worship with a soca rhythm
And a random shout from our Mother Mcgowan
Curious folk from the church's past
Some placing bets how long I'd last

Seventeen years of trial and error
Of Mother Hall saying you're getting better and better
Seventeen years of blessing babies,
Of ageing folk going off to glory.
Seventeen years I can't get back
Friendships formed I'll never forget
Seventeen years I don't regret
These seventeen years have been the best.

We've had our lows We've seen our highs,
We've watched folk come and had painful goodbyes
Some came for long, while some never stayed
Each one enlarged as new purpose was gained

And then there're the ones that have fallen away
The souls we hold close and continue to pray.
Each month of prayer we kneel interceding

That not long from now we'll see them returning
Our sons and our daughters, our mothers and fathers
A day of rejoicing as they come home to Chrisma

It's bittersweet our near departure
The inner sobs, the fits of laughter
The lingering hugs, the smudged mascara.
The call anew another chapter.
It's not goodbye but see you later
It's time to leave my beloved Chrisma.

You are the whole church, reaching the whole person the whole year
The serving church that serves with care
An Indestructible Hope and Faith
With A heart for justice, enabling change.
All these things you are and more
All you've become as you've served our poor.

I'll look to see what next you'll do
As destiny calls for that something new
As millennials become the grown up lot
And the next generation comes and blows up their spot.
I guess what I'm saying is I'll never forget you
And though we move on there's a bond that I'll hold to.
And yes there'll be other churches I pastor
But My first love and favourite will always be Chrisma.

June Golding

A tribute my children's nursery teacher on her retirement.

I was the flustered dad on the first day of nursery
You were the calming voice in my abject misery
"We're new to England", I kind of protested
"She'll be just fine", you gently insisted
Because You were Miss Golding

Not just my children's teacher
A listening ear, a prayer partner
Me you and Miss Reid locked in a cupboard
Bawling our eyes out, crying please help Lord
The passionate June Golding

Samara's grown she's now at Uni
Zephan's five foot ten and climbing
You told me then they'd turn out splendid
And because you did I never doubted
The dependable Miss Golding

This truly is the end of an era
Those story sacks with the hungry caterpillar.
The thought of you leaving it causes us pain
A wonderful friend, June of Dalmain
The lovable adorable unforgettable Miss Golding

I Just Cant Breathe

The public killing of George Floyd was a watershed moment for the whole world. Numbed by this painful ordeal the following was penned.

Death by asphyxiation a modern day execution
Another Black body lays lifeless on our streets.
Another death statistic we've had to concede
Of all the things you may have achieved
Your final words are
I Just Can't Breathe

What's the point of surrender if I'm going to be killed
Say yes sir, no ma'am keep my hands on the wheel.
I'd rather go fighting, than begging to be freed.
I'd rather be upright than drop to my knees
Because whatever my decision
I still can't breathe

Bob says "my hand was made strong by the hand of the Almighty"
Hands of creativity now handcuffed behind me
Hundreds of years still shackled in slavery
Hundreds of years
And I just can't breathe

One pandemic and we're led to panic
Sermons of doom and the end of the planet
Doctrines of vaccines and Mark of the Beast
While Black lives scream loudly
I just can't breathe

My generation has somehow failed
To speak truth to power for fear of being jailed.
We're upset, we're angry and at times we're aggrieved
But statuses on Facebook, Instagram, Twitter, will not help us breathe.

And now we come to our brothers name
More than a colour, a type or a BAME.
I am George Floyd who was crushed by your knee
You'll remember my name as you will my plea
Liberated, exonerated I am now free
Released from your grasp
I can finally breathe

Pentecost

A celebratory piece marking several years of the New Testament Church of God's Pentecostal presence in the United Kingdom.

From an upper room in Jerusalem to a livery stable in Azusa,
To makeshift huts in Jamaica and finally the U.K. diaspora.
Came a Pentecostal fire,
The birthing of revival.
The Comforter had come

Glossolalia, euphoria, psychotic hysteria?
This tongue talking phenomena brought change to the area.
Ushering in a new era
Young and old worshipping together regardless of colour.
Preaching with power converting the sinner
The Paraclete had come

The wind of change blew forcefully
Breathing new life into clergy revitalising laity
Lifting the skirts of conformity, exposing the sin apathy.
Rekindling love and harmony
The Ruach wind had come.

The fire of God was falling,
As grown men held their faces bawling,
Little children no more than ten prophesying, as services went on into the early morning,
A wave of glory now dawning.
Pentecost had come

Pentecostal Movement where is your blaze, has it become a flicker?
Are your golden embers, poignant reminders, that we must retrieve the fire?
Return to the brazen altar?
That upper room inferno?

May Pentecost return.

And so as we prepare to FINISH,
strong in the Spirit's bidding
A second wind is blowing our sons and daughters are praying.
A new generation rising with healing in their tweets.
With the prophetic on their PAGES, they lay prostrate on faces,
Preaching in cyber spaces, reaching untouched places, reaping a global HARVEST
And Pentecost, not as we know it, surely has returned.

Jogging While Black

Another response to the unlawful killing of a young Black man, simply going for a run in the wrong neighbourhood.

Jogging while Black the new reason for attack
For leaving home and never coming back, our brother Ahmaud.
The Bettys the Karens and now the McMichaels
How "dear" a brother go running in the midst of hunting season.

Jogging while Black is no longer a past time regardless of lockdown or any other reason.
If only we'd warned you, from a child drilled it in to you
You're a nigger not a man with a gun pointed at you.

Jogging while Black what's this world slowly coming to
When people of colour can run where they want to.
Be uppity and brave when they're being spoken down to.
Son get your gun, we'll show him who runs things.

Jogging while Black and there's hardly an outrage
Platitudes of prayers but nothing to upstage.
No cries of injustice from the people in Brunswick.
Expressions of anger only seen on a Black face
A mother in turmoil still finding the courage

Jogging while Black is now reserved for the track, the basketball court or the football tarmac
In some prison yard where orange is the new Black
Other than that you could get shot
Whether in Georgia in New York or in the White House.

Tribute to Dad

Phillip Benjamin Grandison
Born in Jamica, Wirefence, Trelawny
16/3/23 - 1/4/19

I see you, Phillip Benjamin Grandison, labourer, carpenter, farmer,
Great husband to Dassa, awesome father to me and my brother Roger.
Grandad to Zephan and Samara.
Son to Israel and Rachel, from the almost obscure village of Wirefence
Trelawny you came,
This fine specimen of men descended upon humanity and rose to great acclaim.

I see you then as a young twenty something,
You visited America trying your hand at farm working.
Then in the early 50's you in your 30's travelled some 4000 miles to England and the rest they say is history.

I can see you now, dusty work clothes after a hard days labour
Hands calloused from years of Britain's cold winter weather.
Racing down to 129 Purves Rd in your green Ford Cortina then years later your mustard Rover
Yep you were a don gorgon driver.

I see you now in Thompson Town Jamaica
Fork in one hand yam tick pan "shoula"
You are the original Missa Massa
Eighty years plus and still a farmer.
Mr Grandy, Sir G, Mas Dada.

I look at you now with your slender frame.
Gentle eyes that seem to say
"Sons I'm so glad you came"
Your speech is slow your voice is very low

But your pride, your pride is high as you look at us and smile.
A fimme bwoy dem yah an dem full a style.

I kiss your head and shave your face as I lift you gently into place.
They say once a man and twice a child
But you are twice the man that I or any man I know can claim to be.
Mas Shortie, head and shoulders above his community, example of love and forgiveness to his family.

I see you now all dressed in white
All blessed and bright
No Parkinson's cancer or diabetes in sight.
You have that look in your eye
That says, "just a little while and there'll be no more goodbyes" as you turn and wave goodbye into that sweet by and by.
Where those gone before welcome you with smiles
Dad we'll see you in a while

Alpha and Beta

To Garrick and Naomi wedded 7/5/24.

You lead she follows
You pour she swallows
You talk she listens
You balk she insists
You're stronger she's weaker
You're alpha she's beta

Alpha and beta, so much better together
None more than the other
Yet weaker without her.
The alpha goes first puts seed in the ground
beta preserves and gives birth over time.

We all love an alpha always getting things done
But your beta makes sure what's done stays done
They ask the right questions though awkward at times
Crossing every t and dotting every i

Warrior alpha the ultimate hunter gatherer and perfect partner
Unless you're stuck in a maze you can't get out of
Then a beta is better

If you stay in your lanes then more work will be done
But lanes sometimes merge and the road becomes one
I guess there are times when the roles are reversed
A change in the order for beta not worse
Each one adapting and learning their course
Poetry in motion as each becomes versed

Alpha and beta, so much better together
A yoking of grace a bonding of lovers

Walking in sync not dragging each other
Going further not faster as you travel together
Learning to yield and not feel lesser
Taking the lead and yet being graceful.

You're Alpha big A and Omega big O
Directing our actions, sustaining our souls
Two separate entities, yet one distinct whole
More fulfilling purpose than playing a role
A waltz of surrender and not of control
An inseparable Union the ultimate goal.

Simon Says

A dear friend gone too soon, continue to rest in peace.
10/5/69 - 27/12/23

Simon says there's work to do
No time to waste or think it through
Simon says let's spread the word
And soon in clubs, His name was heard.

Simon says let's move the world
Simon says let's move us first
Simon dared to be the change
Simon cared and was the change

Simon oft would make us smile
Just point his lens and wait a while
Black and white or glorious colour
Our lived out memories held forever

Simon says I'll come and see you
Have a chat and catch up with you
Simon says wow it's 2am, we'll have to meet and chat again.
3am still by the door, Simon says we'll talk some more.

Simon says my bodies weak, my kidneys fail but still I speak
Simon says what's your excuse
A healthy life he's yet to use
Simon says don't wait too late
Your words could change another's fate

Simon says it's time to go
No last goodbyes no fake excuse
What's done is done, the rest you'll do
To thine own self you must be true.

Simon says I've done my best
Simon says I've no regrets
Simon asks have I passed the test?
Jesus says come home and rest.

Sarai

Dedicated to my honorary granddaughter, continue to make us proud.

I remember you came a precocious tot
Funny, vibrant and talking a lot.
Each Sunday morning we'd pick you both up.
And take you to Chrisma your brand new church home

You and I both born in March
Your shady comments "mum don't feel bad"
The look you gave someone asking change from a fiver
When raising funds for poor kids in Africa

I remember our lunch at a local Harvester
You being excited and your mum getting sterner
A short trip to the loo, you returned less animated
With Nikki composed as if nothing had transpired

You and mum, Nikki and Sarai
Partners in life, both low and both high
You looked to her and she to you
To be your best selves whatever you went through.
All these I remember

I remember the morning we immersed you in water
A most natural step in your walk as a believer
Your testimony of faith it blew us away
As you shared how the Lord had showed you the way

I remember mum saying you'd both be leaving
I remember the sadness and joy we were feeling.
I remember not coming to the airport that day
Unable to face our parting of ways

Then all these years later to see you grown
Beauty and brilliance all rolled up in one
The Sarai I knew has not been lost
Just older and wiser and doing the most

So my prayer for you our Princess Sarai
Is that the fire within you will never die
I pray your passion for life, grow brighter and brighter
I pray you'll succeed and go higher and higher
I pray you'll lead as well as you've followed.
Your portion of blessings be doubled and doubled
I pray you'll pray and your prayers be listened to
I pray you'll remember the things that shaped you.

Liburd Baby Onboard

To Esther and Mark your visit that evening was so inspiring, this is for little Reign.

Liburd baby onboard, a gift in response to a word
A blessing to a prayer that was heard
A testimony of earnest preserve
The fruit of unconditional love

Liburd baby onboard, the one thing she isn't is bored
Those kicks and turns and the occasional heartburn
Makes you even more loved and much more adored

Liburd baby onboard, this baby is certainly with it
Saying amen from the womb when mum's exhorting
Quickening when dad's teaching
This child be coming out straight preaching.

Liburd baby onboard, we anxiously await your birth
The sound of your cry in the Earth
A sound that says you're here
A sound we've all been waiting to hear.

Liburd baby onboard, you fill up my world
Daily redefining my meaning and worth
In the company of friends I feel you reel
And in the presence of some you go eerily still.

Liburd baby onboard, your father and I we give you our word
One that you'll always be heard and not herd
Number one even though you were third.
We promise you'll ever be loved
And ensure that you're always onboard.

The Blood Cries Out

A cry for justice for the many lives cut short whilst I served as minister in West Croydon.

Beef in the streets and none on the table
Pie in the sky won't cut it in Croydon
Man dem making bread for some bacon.
Living the dream of a nightmare situation
Look at my drip, all dripping and bloody
The Blood cries out loud a bradda just whet me

The Blood cries out from your nan's front garden
It's cries out loud from a tenth floor landing, a stairwell
in Peckham, in Deptford, in Croydon.
It cries out help but no one's listening
A mum cries out from the loss she's feeling.

Like child soldiers recruited for a pointless war
Olders grooming youngers and so on and so on.
Absent fathers who've let the side down
Enabling mothers that are hiding the guns.
Chaotic homes where everyone shouts
These are the things that the blood cries out.

No time for photo opportunities
As journalist vultures circle our communities
Huge black mics with phallic like obsession
Probing lenses with voyeuristic intentions.
Twisting quotes like my sis's extensions
Ignoring the cries of my bloody condition

Churches are marching, the mosques over crowding,
Bobbies on the beat are beating
But the blood's still crying.

How many young will we have to bury
Before we go up stream and address the bleeding
Call out politicians who are just too greedy
Where the blood first cried out "somebody failed me"
Do you have this problem on your high street.
Cross the road for every stranger you meet.
Is your lad stopped by police every week
Or is it just My Ends where the crying won't cease

The blood cries out, "my brother 'slayed' me"
All in the name of a postcode I'm caged in
A place of abject poverty
Fighting a war of futility
A turf soaked in the life God gave me
"Wasted" cries the blood of a teen aged prodigy

These streets are ours and we must reclaim it
Like INSULATE let's glue ourselves to it.
Let's make a plan and then all stick to it.
Let's Turn chicken shops into workshops
Bookies into youth clubs
And church halls into nutrition hubs
That's what the blood cries out

Let's stop fighting for funding and discover the fun
doing what's worth doing
Let's put fat cats on a slimming programme.
Help poor Kat put some weight on
Spend more time with her struggling son Jayden
Let's tell the MET that we're not all louts
Just a few of the things the blood cries out

The blood cries out "who's going to be next"
"Who'll avenge my death by making a change"

As the blood of our children cry out for healing
Let's remember the dead and not neglect the living
The only blood shed should be that which we're giving
The only cries heard should be that of rejoicing

Why I'm Staying in the New Testament Church of God

In celebration of those who arrived in the United Kingdom in the 1950's from the Caribbean and other warm places, overcoming various challenging scenarios.

They were a culture within a culture.
To many a freak of nature a throwback of Puritan fervour.
But deep down inside her
They just loved the saviour.

Not only did they look Holy with their flamboyant hats and modest dress
they lived it seven days a week as they gave the world their best.

You could spot them on the trains and buses embracing Monday morning,
still lashed, sorry blessed by the three points of Sunday's sermon.
How could you tell how did you know
Well besides their lipstick-less lips and lack of eye shadow,
they had that glow

The women ranged from factory workers to social workers,
nurses and bus conductors.
Some were office clerks in the council for it's perks.
Healthcare assistants and primary school teachers, cleaners,
hairdressers and aspiring students.

The men, they were home bred providers, Caribbean outliers
They were decorators, builders, repairers, not just of cars and
houses but their newly come brothers.
They were domino players, the original game readers and if you
were unlucky to get six love, the biggest teasers.

But come Sunday they were all one
No one was better than anyone.
Your table was my table and so was your bed.
Until pastor took the mic you'd never have guessed that he was the head.

They had all things common without being common
They worshipped God, not people, not mammon.
In the fifties we came and they received us not
But if we're really honest the CofE and Baptists just weren't hot.
If you're born in the fire you can't live in mere smoke
And so if your eyes have been opened, you've no choice but to be woke.

I came in the 90's when our Conventions were glorious De Montfort
and Brighton as we sang out chorus after chorus.
Mighty men and women some passed and gone
Have laid a foundation we must stand and build on.

On through the hard times on through change
On through heartache and on through blame.
I cannot leave though often tempted
I will not leave though pews be emptied.

Our past is great but our God is greater.
And if Job is correct so is our latter
Rather than hate and be it's accuser
With fondness and affection I'll turn and praise her.
Giving thanks to our God for His uncommon favour

How I Got Over

In celebration of those who arrived in the United Kingdom in the 1950's from the Caribbean and other warm places, overcoming various challenging scenarios.

Grip in one hand fate in the other
We land at Southampton on a damp November
Sun-less skies and smog all over
Begins the story of how we got over.

In those few frantic moments as we braved the crowd
Was the voice of my uncle shouting my name out loud
A huge warm coat gently placed on my shoulders.
The kindness of family that brought me over.

Where are the leaves that cover the trees
No flowers, no plants, no birds no bees
The cold has gone from my "foot" to my knees
An icy cold wind for my island breeze.

If the weather was cold the people were colder.
The looks and the stares made it even more "wusurer"
Just five more years and it'll all be over
The thoughts of home I couldn't get over.

As time went on we got into a groove
On Saturday nights we started to groove
For some on Sundays the Spirit would move
Then come Monday morning we'd be back in the groove.

Our children were born and some came over
Rough at first but we smoothed things over
The sounds of joy and infectious laughter;
Of family and friends is how we got over.

Our national conventions were our yearly Mecca
When God would move and His Spirit take over
In De Montfort Hall or the Brighton Centre
Singing loudly on those coaches, is how we got over.
We got over our loss through times of prayer
We met in homes and worshipped Jehovah
A brilliant word in our darkest hour
Is how time and time we all got over.

As the years go by so many have crossed over
Gone to rest from their toil and their labour
We'll join them soon if not for the rapture
Gathered round the throne in the great hereafter
Our faith in God and love for each other
Tells the wonderful story of how we got over

Our Story Retold

The retelling of the sad story of slaves during the transatlantic trade and where they are today.

Ours is a story not often retold
How strangers in big ships came seeking our gold
And we being trusting then loosened our hold
Were loaded on big ships and placed in its hold

Graded degraded, shackled and traded
A child and her mother like cattle paraded.
A father and son that are now separated
While cousins and aunties in the oceans were "drownded"

Sold to the man in the big broad hat
A few hundred dollars and a bargain at that.
Our esteemed forefathers never bargained for that
A few hundred years and we're still paying the debt

We worked their plantations
Creating scandalous amounts of wealth
Breast feeding white babies
Whilst ours lacked good health.
Mothers drowning babies so they wouldn't live as slaves

When finally they freed us with the promise of land
A mule, 40 acres and a chance to belong.
They snared us with laws that would make us go wrong
Stifled our dreams and muted our song
Of freedom

We created our Wall Street
And built our own towns
Til jealous marauders

Came and burnt it all down
White hooded men and a burning cross
Enraged by Black excellence and the line we dared cross

In 2008 you crowned us king
We lived in your White House with our ebony skin.
Then came the hate and a deluge of lies
But as Maya A said yet still we rise and rise.

As this chapter ends and another begins
Amidst the trauma and most racist of sins
There's a blood stained cry for something that's new
A call for true justice from the unmarked tombs.

Ours is a story not often retold
How strangers from big ships conquered their new world
Survived against odds unbelievably skewed
A people displaced, a people renewed

Three Young Lions

The story of how Marcus Rashford, Jadon Sancho and Bukayo Saka were vilified by the press in the 2021 Euros.

Three young lions in the Euros final
Three brave men now lambs to the slaughter
Three young brothers in the midst of hyenas
Modern day gladiators in a virtual arena

The looks of fear, of shock then shame
As faceless cowards decry their names
Such racist tropes over a simple game
But the three young lions remain the same.

They came as cubs to your football clubs
Made you money by scoring goals
Calling them niggers won't change their worth
A lion's a lion right from its very birth.

Sick and tired of seeing me score?
Brace yourselves lads, there's a whole lot more
300 lions getting ready to roar
3 million brothers outside your door

Doors of industry and not just sport
Roars of victory when one wins the vote.
These lions are hungry to see justice won
Feeding the poor like what Rashford done.

Bigging up mothers and buying them houses
Remembering young kids and building them centres
The days of holding us bound in irons
Have come to an end because of our Lions

These three lions belong to us
Rashford Saka and our boy Sancho
Touch one of them and you touch us all
Keep up your nonsense and we'll leave with our ball
Fifty five years to get this far
Decades of failure resting on three stars
We didn't win but you all are winners
To all Young Lions the future is in us.

You Are The Chosen

A tribute to the late Rev Dr Joel Edwards a mentor and friend.

When He needed a man to show a man
He looked in your direction
An ordinary man but a willing man
It's clear that you were chosen

A boy who did what other boys did
Some we've shared and some we hid.
A young man flawed but never floored
The cryptic writings were on the wall

You played in bands but not the fool
You suffered pangs but never fools
In crowded marches on picket lines
Free Mandela and women's rights
Chosen! A man ahead of his time

You showed a way how "church" could be.
Set a standard for the likes of me
And yet to some you lowered the standard of what was Holy
Women in trousers and jewellery.
Oh Lord have mercy pan me soul an body.

Sealed from conception, destined to lead your generation
A world view beyond your education
Crossing cultures and denomination
Convincing "them" that we weren't all morons
It's clear that you were chosen.

Funny and witty you made us laugh somewhat nervously
As if the joke might be on me
That real change started with me

That people attained only to what they could see
For such a time He chose you.
We were proud to call you son
We played the fool and you were gone
Despite the threats you kept your tongue
You are indeed the chosen one

And now we learn another lesson
The look of grace while facing cancer
The sound of faith through tears and laughter
Ding ding round two
We see why God did choose you.

We see you sweating drips of blood
We hear you giving glory to God
Your flesh is mouthing "Let it pass from me"
Your spirit retorting "Let it be unto me. Whatever will be will be.
We share these thoughts for the things you've done
And sit at your feat oh chosen one

We all awoke to the saddening news
Our friend had passed on the last of June
If we had chosen you'd not be gone
But the one who chose you called you home.
And because He's sovereign in all He's done
We release you Joel to the faithful One.

You said what you said: a modern day mash up of Psalms 91 & 73

Written in the heart of the pandemic the writer was desperately trying to make sense of the devastation around and his resolve to lean on the Psalms as a place of comfort.

You said no plague would come nigh our dwelling
No noisome pestilence
If you were our covering
We look in our world and doom is pending
But you said what you said despite what I'm feeling.

You walked the earth and the dead were raised
Lepers healed as multitudes grazed
Today there's disease and famine instead
And despite what I'm feeling you said what you said

Where are these angels you've sent from your throne
My feet bleed profusely as they're dashed against stones
Adders and lions they swallow me whole
But you said what you said
So let your will be done.

I've confessed your word
Told myself I believed
I've turned to my neighbour
Declared and decreed
Played spiritual casino and called it a seed
But you said what you said
And I'll trust you indeed.

If I'm totally honest my feet almost slipped
As the wicked they prospered and got on with their tricks.
But I waited for Sunday and you gave me a glimpse

How justice was meted
Because you said what you said.

So I'll believe what you said
And remain Spirit led
Abandon the voices of hurt in my head
Feelings birthed from my limited stead
And despite what I'm seeing, hearing feeling
I'll believe what you said.

You are the Father

A Father's Day tribute, celebrating the men who do an awesome job in raising the next generation.

Young single and carefree, married with three, widowed and elderly, the test results say, you are the father.
Planned or unplanned, delighted or sad,
Hey, the kid looks just like ya.

Loved or hated, present or incarcerated, praised, berated, you are the father.
Whether you stepped in, stepped out or stepped up, you are the father.
Even if the kid looks nothing like ya.

Employed, deployed, devoid, annoyed, avoid...ed,
You are the father.
Strict or Light hearted, ailing or dearly departed, you are the father.
And yes this kid still loves ya.

Flawed or floored, retreated or forward, your steps are followed, your significance honoured,
Because you "are" the father.
And awesome as she is with her red "kickers", a mother could never be father,
Even if the kid acts just like her.

Living the word or living in the world, you are the father.
Father to your own and the ones you decided to own or doing it all on your own,
You a bad mother father, sole breadwinner, holding it all together.
An a you de yute fava.

Two jobs and a side hustle you put food on the table
A kick about in the park when you're able
You are the father.
You get angry, you calm down, you embrace, you smile,

You are the father.
And the kid believes in ya.

Holy, hallowed, heavenly
You are the Father, ultimate designer consummate provider.
Your DNA, Divine Nature and Ability, your supernatural acuity,
all displayed in us beautifully.
Who but God could be the Father.
And your kids wanna be just like ya.

Anymore

A response to the death of another black civilian by police in the U.S.

I don't know what's right anymore
Daunte Wright ain't here anymore
Daunte's rights ain't fair anymore
I really can't sing from this sheet anymore

You taser taser tase me
Then bleep bleep you say you shot me
Ain't nothing holy about that $#!% Miss Police lady
Ain't no BCPD gonna pay to
raise my baby.

I'm not quite sure if I ocare anymore
What you think of me and the same old score
Our cry of injustice against the poor
Your abuse of power on Adam Toledo

Thirteen years old and he's such a huge threat
Despite your guns and a bullet proof vest.
With two hands raised, two shots to the chest.
Another mistake another Black child dead.

That's it I can't be quiet anymore
Preach about heaven with this hell at my door
Teach about healing and turning my cheek
While Black men lie handcuffed face down in the street.

I really don't want to hear it anymore
Your gaslighting sermons as if nothing is wrong.
It's time for a different kind of hermeneutic
Texts that read like a modern day classic.

It's time for a whole new political agenda
One about race and not just about gender.
It's time for the people to all come together
The quiet revolution to suddenly get louder.

Like Jeremiah I said, I wouldn't preach anymore
Just get on with my day job and not rock the boat
But the more I hear the sighs and the groans
Is the more I feel the fire in my bones.
Son of man can these bones live anymore
Indeed if the people will care once more

I Will Not Unfriend You

A lighthearted look at addressing disagreements on social media and otherwise.

I will not unfriend you remove or pretend you...
Don't exist
Just because you
hold a different point of view
Defend what I deem to be untrue
I won't Unfriend you

If you worship on Sunday in JESUS name
Or praise on the Sabbath I'll love you the same.
If your SUNDAY SERVICE has lights and a smoke machine
If your ladies wear hats and knock a tambourine
I won't Unfriend you

If your mind is unstable by the pressures of life
Your body disabled by cancerous mites
If you've lost in love because you failed to be true
I'll draw close to you if you permit me too
But I will not Unfriend you

I won't get the hump if you voted Trump
Want to remain or adore Kanye
I won't Unfriend you
If you've fallen from grace and become a disgrace
Use expletives because you're losing your faith
I won't Unfriend you

What I will not do, is lie to you
Say "yes it's true" just to be friends with you
I may throw shade as I'm known to do
But I won't throw dirt

And I won't Unfriend you

Speak truth to power and then let it simmer
Say nothing at all if that suits you better.
You may choose to differ or maybe defer
Say what you like or what you prefer
I still won't Unfriend you

It's not that deep and not that serious
The squabbles we're having are kind of hilarious
While we're downloading tracks and buying the T-shirt
Defending your boy another boy got murdered
Someone we could have friended.

If you log on to Facebook and can't see my page
Check on Insta and can't see updates
I'm still friends with you
I actually still love you
Enough to not always be arguing with you
Constantly berating you and not seeing the Christ in you
I will not Unfriend you.

The Master Pastor

To Bishop Malcolm Cummins
On the occasion of his Appreciation Service
Claion B Grandison
19th January 2020

My dearest friend my prayer partner
My confidante, my secret mentor
You are a master pastor

You serve with grace
You serve in haste
Forever busy
Hence sometimes late
Still you are the master pastor

In times of sorrow
In times of death
You leave the warmth of your King sized bed
To ensure the saints are comforted
The selfless Master Pastor

You have a laugh
Though poor at jokes
You're different strokes to different folks
Yep you're that kind of bloke
Bishop Malcolm aka The Master Pastor

For all the years I've known you sir
You've never said an unkind word
Never failed to put folks first
Expects the best and never the worst (Especially if it's in a red shirt)
The patient Long-suffering, Liverpool supporting Master Pastor

Ten years from now or maybe twenty
I pray your store basket be filled with plenty
Your jugs of joy may not be empty
Maureen the kids and grandkids all healthy

The fruitful Master Pastor

Black Lives Matter

A response to the famous Black Lives Matter March that took place simultaneously all over the world, involving people young and old, gay straight, Black and White.

Black lives matter, the blacker the better?
The chants grow louder as the crowds get wider and whiter?
Megaphones blasting, millennials kneeling
Buildings burning
A militant brand of policing

Black lives matter from the cradle, gay straight or disabled.
Before you lay on that table
Remember pro-life, pro choice is just a label
Black and brown children sweating for our cherished designer labels
Black lives in prison designing your designer table

Black lives matter
Child soldiers in modern Africa
Trafficked lives in Nigeria
Bring Back Our Girls a forgotten mantra
While three cops walk free for killing our beloved Breonna Taylor

Black lives matter in the church you pastor
The token Black life that sits on your choir
That committed Black life so faithful in prayer
Who's good for a laugh but not for your daughter.

All lives matter, so what's the matter
What's the big deal if my skin is lighter
When it all boils down it's a matter of matter
Unless of course you don't ever see colour
Black lives matter! misunderstood or grave misnomer

Black lives matter
Attacked lives matter
Central Park Five lives still do matter
Black "Red Lined" lives in "urban designs"
Black segregated schools teaching segregated minds do matter

May my Black life matter til it gets in your face
Go up your left nostril and drain out your right ear
May you never overlook
what's unique to me
lump me in a BAME
or gaslight my view

Black lives matter young, female, old
Murdered by police while asleep in their homes.
Neighbourhood watched as you make your way home
Shot dead in the streets as "he" stood his ground.
Black lives a matter we must all encounter
The sooner the better or the worse our encounter
As MJ says we must look in the mirror
Not a casual glance or a fleeting endeavour
Not holding a sign or wearing a T-shirt
But holding a gaze as you dissect your character.

Black lives mattered as we entered the hold
Shackled in fetters from our African homes
Four months of "lockdown" and you're losing your minds
Try four hundred years of trying and trying

When we pull down your statues and put ours there
We're not trying to take over, we're saying we're here.
Afro hair and clenched fist in the air
Black Lives Matter we're here to declare

ABOUT THE BOOK

Our Story Retold is the long awaited anthology of the author's first series of poetry. Bishop Claion's art has always been evident in his sermons as he is known for his creative and vivid ways in portraying characters along with his play on words, or "Clai-on words", as one person puts it. Our Story Retold is unapologetically Black in its essence but universal in its significance. Each poem captures the lived challenges and victories experienced by Black people as a collective. This unique work began in 2018 as the author experimented with various styles of writing (thanks to Veniesha). However, the catalyst of the vision for a book was the civil and social events during and after the Covid-19 pandemic as the author used his writing as a means and voice to build conversation and motivate others to contend with the issues and be an advocate for change. Our Story Retold is also a celebration of Black excellence and a recognition of the indomitable focus of a people that often influences achievements at exponential levels that outpaces systemic struggles. We hope you'll enjoy this great work as much as the author enjoyed writing it, and that you will be inspired and empowered to play your part in shaping and preserving a people.

LEAVE A REVIEW ON AMAZON

If you have enjoyed reading this book, kindly leave a review on Amazon as this will enable the author to reach other potential readers.

Thank you!

ABOUT THE AUTHOR

Claion Grandison is the Administrative Bishop of the New Testament Church of God in England & Wales and has been in full time ministry since 2000. Over the years his engagement with individuals within and outside the Faith community has given a unique gift of capturing life with radical sensitivity. Though born in North London Claion spent his early years growing up on the politically and economically complex but vibrant and charming island of Jamaica. Having experienced poverty himself, the author is no stranger to hardship and the angst associated with that lifestyle. Caringly and carefully Claion draws on these and many other wonderful experiences to bring to you his very first offering, Our Story Retold. He has been married to Sonia for 30 years, they have two adult children, Samara and Zephan.

CONNECT WITH CLAION B. GRANDISON

For more on Claion Grandison's upcoming books
and projects follow him on social media:

Made in the USA
Middletown, DE
07 November 2024

63657207R00056